Where is the Bear?

Words by Camilla de la Bédoyère

Illustrations by Emma Levey

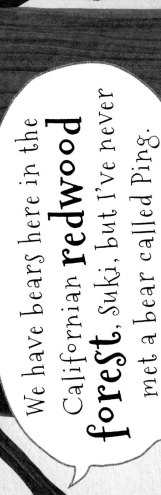

We have bears here in the Californian **redwood forest**, Suki, but I've never met a bear called Ping.

If you're not Ping, who are you?

I'm an **American black bear**. I'm tearing bark off this tree so I can find juicy bugs hiding underneath!

If you match the animals to their descriptions you will reach an owl who may be able to help. I'm a **yellow-cheeked chipmunk**. I climb trees to find insects, seeds, leaves, nuts and flowers to eat. I live in a cosy burrow at the foot of this tree.

I'm striped to warn that I can sting.
My busy buzz is how I sing.
What am I?

Do you like my fancy feathers? Pigeons live all over the world, but have you ever seen a gorgeous **green pigeon** like me?

I am a **peacock** and my tail feathers have colourful patterns called eye-spots on them. If I had ten tail feathers with three eye-spots on each, how many eye-spots would I have altogether?

Suki, these ants have got a clue for you. Come and have a look.

Look how long my claws are! I use them to rip open ants' nests – I can eat thousands of ants at a time! I'm a **sloth bear**, and I carry my baby on my back.

Turn the page Suki!

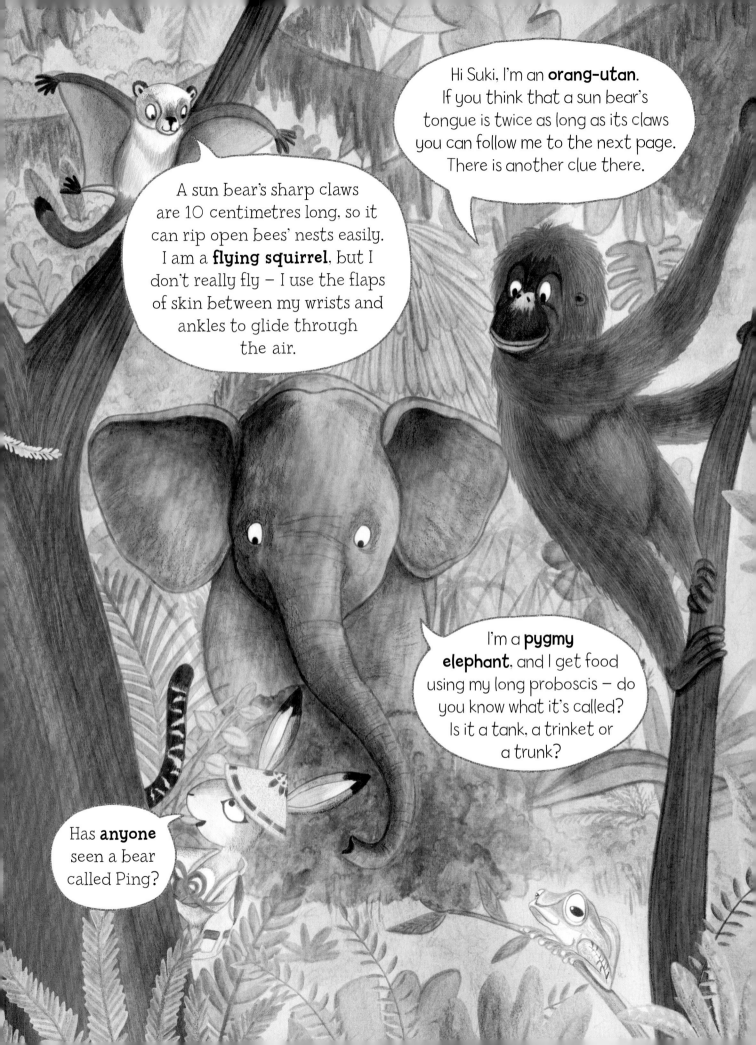

COOL CONIFER FORESTS:
THE TREES HAVE NEEDLE-LIKE LEAVES. BEARS THAT LIVE HERE HIBERNATE IN THE WINTER.

WOODLAND:
COOLER AND DRIER THAN A RAINFOREST. BROWN BEARS AND BLACK BEARS LIVE HERE.

BAMBOO FOREST:
WARM IN THE SUMMER, COLD IN WINTER. PING LIVES HERE.

TROPICAL RAINFOREST:
HOT AND RAINY. SUN BEARS LIVE HERE.

Suki has met polar bears, black bears, brown bears (including grizzlies), sun, sloth and moon bears. I think there is one type of bear she hasn't met yet. Can you guess what type of bear Ping might be?

These little ones are very playful, but they don't seem to be concentrating on their lesson! I think I've spotted a useful clue. Now I know where I'll find Ping!